Won't You Be My KISSAROO?

JOANNE RYDER   MELISSA SWEET

SCHOLASTIC INC.

New York Toronto London Auckland Sydney
Mexico City New Delhi Hong Kong Buenos Aires

ISBN-13: 978-0-545-03013-7
ISBN-10: 0-545-03013-7

Text copyright © 2004 by Joanne Ryder
Illustrations copyright © 2004 by Melissa Sweet
All rights reserved. Published by Scholastic Inc., 557 Broadway, New York, NY 10012,
by arrangement with Harcourt, Inc. SCHOLASTIC and associated logos are trademarks
and/or registered trademarks of Scholastic Inc.

12 11 10 9 8 7 6 5 4 3 2 1   7 8 9 10 11/0

Printed in the U.S.A.   40

This edition first printing, March 2007

The illustrations in this book were created in watercolor, pencil, and collage.
The display type was set in Colwell.
The text type was set in Mercurius Light.
Designed by Lydia D'moch

To Larry, my dear kissaroo
—J. R.

To Henry
—M. S.

Won't you be my *kissaroo*?
I've lots of kisses just for you.

A morning kiss is full of sun
and wishes for the day to come.

A breakfast kiss is nice and sweet.
It's fun when sticky lips can meet.

A good-bye kiss goes with a hug
to keep you safe and feeling snug.

A hello kiss is soft as rain.
It's good to see your face again.

A puppy kiss is very wet,
as silly as a kiss can get.

A kitten kiss is just a lick,
a friendly touch, so light and quick.

A playful kiss will often squeak
and make a **POP!** upon your cheek.

A gotcha kiss surprises you
with tickles and some giggles, too.

A birthday kiss, while candles glow,
will make you **grow**

and **grow**

and **grow**

A bedtime kiss will tuck you tight
and keep you cozy through the night.

So...
Won't you be my kissaroo?
And every day, the whole day through,
we'll share *new* kisses...

...me and you!